299

THIS BOOK BELONGS
TO
Janice fisher
You are my best
friend.
FROM
Love
Camille
Cushing

DANNY

KAYE'S
STORIES
FROM
FARAWAY
PLACES

RANDOM HOUSE, NEW YORK

Thanks are extended to the following authors, publishers, translators, and organizations for allowing the use of their stories in this book:

THE RABBIT'S CLEVER NOSE is from "The Rabbit Has a Cold" in *Burmese Folk Tales* by Maung Htin Aung. Copyright by Oxford University Press, Bombay, 1948.

SINDBAD AND THE OLD MAN OF THE SEA is adapted from Richard F. Burton's *Arabian Nights*. Adaptation © 1960 by Anne Ross.

THE IMAGINARY WEDDING, copyright © 1960 by Margaret Bevans and Barbara Klaw, is based on a summary of a story by Wadia Shatara of Jordan and is printed with her permission.

A GUEST FOR HALIL, is reprinted from *Once the Hodja* by Alice Geer Kelsey, copyright 1943 by permission of Longmans, Green & Co.

THE DONKEY AND THE ROCK is by A. L. Shelton.

BASTIANELO, copyright © 1960 by Margaret Bevans and Barbara Klaw, is adapted from a story by T. F. Crane.

PIPILO is adapted from Margaret Hasluck's *Albanian-English Reader*, Cambridge University Press, 1932. By permission of the publisher. Adaptation copyright © 1960 by Margaret Bevans and Barbara Klaw.

THE CONCEITED SPIDER is slightly adapted from *West African Folk Tales* by W. H. Barker and C. Sinclair, reproduced by permission of George G. Harrap & Co., Ltd., London.

THE SILLY FELLOW WHO SOLD HIS BEARD is reprinted by permission of the publishers, the Vanguard Press, from *The Gypsies' Fiddle and Other Gypsy Stories* by M. A. Jagendorf and C. H. Tillhagen. Copyright 1956 by M. A.

Jagendorf and C. H. Tillhagen.

THE RAM AND THE LION'S SON, copyright © 1960 by Margaret Bevans and Barbara Klaw, is based on a story by Sir James E. Alexander.

THE TIGER, THE BRAHMAN, AND THE JACKAL is reprinted from *Indian Fairy Tales* by Joseph Jacobs with the permission of G. P. Putnam's Sons.

THE BRAHMAN'S DREAM is reprinted from *The Panchatantra* translated by Arthur W. Ryder by permission of the University of Chicago Press. Copyright 1925 by the University of Chicago.

THE VEGETABLE TREE is from *Bright* *Feather and Other Mayan Tales* by Dorothy Rhoads. Copyright 1932 by Dorothy Rhoads. Reprinted by permission of Doubleday and Company, Inc.

THE CANDLE IN THE DARKNESS is adapted from "The Candle Gives Out Heat" in *Stories from the Near East* by Leslie W. Leavitt, by permission of Longmans, Green & Co., Ltd., London.

THE FARMER OF BABRIA is from *The Fire on the Mountain and Other Ethiopian Stories* by Harold Courlander and Wolf Leslau. Copyright 1950 by Henry Holt and Company, Inc. By permission of the publishers.

THE RABBIT'S CLEVER NOSE

BURMA: This version of an old tale is by Maung Htin Aung.

KING LION appointed the Bear, the Monkey, and the Rabbit to be his ministers of state, and together they roamed the forest. But one day the Lion became tired of their company, and wanted to kill and eat them. However, as he himself had chosen them to be his ministers, he had to think of an excuse which would give a semblance of legality to his unjust act.

So King Lion called his three ministers of state, and said to them, "My lords, you have been my ministers for some time, and I must now find out whether high office has spoilt you." The Lion opened his mouth wide, and asked the Bear to state what sort of smell ensued from the royal mouth. As the Lion was a great meat-eater, naturally a foul smell came out from his mouth.

The Bear, ever truthful, said, "Your Majesty, it is a foul smell."

"Rank treason," roared the Lion in anger. "You insult the king to his face. The punishment for treason is death." So saying, he pounced upon the Bear and killed him.

The Lion now asked the Monkey to say what sort of smell ensued from the royal mouth. The Monkey, after witnessing the fate of the Bear, thought that the only way to escape with his life was to resort to flattery, and said, "Your Majesty, it is a delicious smell, as sweet as the choicest perfume."

"You are a liar and a flatterer," roared the Lion in anger. "Everyone knows that only a foul smell can come out of my mouth as I am a great meat-eater. Untruthful and flattering counselors to the king are a danger to the state." So saying, he pounced upon the Monkey and killed him.

The Lion now said to the Rabbit, "Wise Rabbit, what sort of smell ensues from my mouth?"

"I am sorry, Your Majesty," replied the Rab-

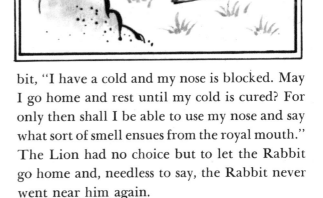

bit, "I have a cold and my nose is blocked. May I go home and rest until my cold is cured? For only then shall I be able to use my nose and say what sort of smell ensues from the royal mouth." The Lion had no choice but to let the Rabbit go home and, needless to say, the Rabbit never went near him again.

And to this day in Burma, when a person is being cagey and won't express an opinion, it is said that "he has a cold!"

SINDBAD AND THE OLD MAN OF THE SEA

IRAQ: Sindbad is a merchant whose seven voyages are described in the *Arabian Nights*. In this story, he tells a friend of one of his adventures.

THE GIANT BIRD Ruhk had crushed our ship with the huge boulder she let fall, and we were all cast into the sea. But Allah sent me one of the planks as I struggled for life and I clung to it, paddling with my feet. The wind and waves bore me to an island and cast me up on the shore where I lay half dead with hunger and thirst.

When I revived and walked about, I found the island was a paradise. Its trees were laden with ripe fruit, its streams ran clear and bright, there were flowers to delight the eye and birds to enchant the ear. So I ate my fill of the fruits and drank from the streams and gave thanks to Allah for my deliverance. And, at nightfall, I lay down and slept as one exhausted.

In the morning, I rose and walked about until I came to a well fed by a running stream.

Crouched beside the well was an old man dressed in a waistcloth of palm frond fiber. I thought he must be one of those who were wrecked on the ship and I drew near him and greeted him courteously, but the old man did not answer except by gestures.

I said to him, "Oh, Uncle, what causeth thee to sit there?"

The old man moaned and signaled to me as if to say, "Take me up on thy shoulders and carry me across the stream."

Thinking he might be ill or crippled, I bent down and took him up on my back and carried him across the stream. Here I leaned over and told him to dismount at his leisure. But he would not get off and instead wound his legs around my neck. They were like a buffalo's hide for roughness and blackness and, fright-

ened, I tried to throw him off. But the old man gripped my neck with his legs until I was nearly choked and the world grew dark to my sight and I fell senseless to the ground. But the old man, still keeping his seat, raised his legs and drummed with his heels on my back and shoulders until I was forced to rise for the pain.

Then he signaled to me with his hand to carry him hither and thither among the trees so that he might pick the best fruits. If I refused or if I went too slowly, he beat me with his feet more grievously than if I had been beaten with whips. So I carried him about the island as if I were a captive slave and he dismounted neither night nor day. When he wished to sleep, he wound his legs about my neck and leaned back and slept awhile, then awoke and beat me so that I sprang up in haste to follow his commands.

As I continued my miserable, weary way, I reproached myself for having felt sorry for him. "I did him a favor and he repays me with ill. By Allah, never more will I do any man a service as long as I live!" I thought. And again and again I wished I might die.

One day I came with him to a place where there were many gourds and some of them were dry. I took a great dry gourd and, cutting open the head, scooped out the inside and cleaned it. Then I gathered grapes from a nearby vine and squeezed them into the gourd until it was full of juice. Then I stopped up the mouth and set it in the sun where I left it for several days until the juice became strong wine. Every day I used to drink of it, and it comforted me and seemed to make my troubles lighter.

One day he saw me drinking and signaled to me as if to ask, "What is that?"

Said I, "It is an excellent cordial which cheers the heart and revives the spirits." Then I began to caper about among the trees, clapping my hands and singing and making merry, and I pretended to stagger under him.

He signaled to me to give him the gourd that he might drink and I gave it to him. So he drained it to the dregs and cast it to the ground. Then he grew merry and began to clap his hands and jig on my shoulders until finally the fumes of the wine overcame him and his leg muscles relaxed and he swayed to and fro on my back.

When I saw that he had lost his senses for drunkenness, I put my hand to his legs and, loosening them from my neck, I threw the devil to the ground where he lay senseless.

After that, I returned to the place where I had landed on the shore and waited, keeping a lookout for passing ships, until one day, behold!, a ship was making for the island through the dashing sea and clashing waves. When the sailors landed, I hailed them and they gathered around me, asking me how I came there.

They marveled as they heard my story and said, "He who rode on thy shoulders is called "Shayk al-Bahr" or "Old Man of the Sea," and no man who has felt those legs on his neck has ever lived until now."

So I gave thanks to Allah, for I knew my escape had been a miracle.

THE IMAGINARY WEDDING

JORDAN, SAUDI ARABIA: Stories about Juha—a man who is often tripped up by his own cunning—are so popular in Arab countries that most Arab children know dozens of them. Based on a story told by Wadia Shatara.

WHEN JUHA finished his shopping at the town market, he was tired and hot. He decided to rest for a while under a large tree before starting home. The tree cast a welcome shade, and he soon began to nod and drowse comfortably.

Soon, however, a group of boys discovered him napping there, and began to tease him.

"Hey, Juha," one small boy shouted, dancing merrily in front of him. "Hey, hey, hey," shouted another, startling Juha by poking his head suddenly around the trunk of the tree behind him.

"Go away, boys," Juha said crossly. "Can't you see I'm sleeping?" This sent the children into peals of laughter, and they danced and teased all the more. Juha decided that if he was to have his nap, he'd have to think of some clever way to get rid of them.

"Why are you wasting your time around here, children?" he said, after thinking for a moment. "Don't you know about the wedding? Don't you want any candy?"

"Candy?" the children said. "What candy? What wedding?"

"Why, everybody knows about it," Juha said. "The whole town's invited, and they are giving free candy to everyone who comes. Surely you must have heard the news. It's at the big house, down at the other end of the village."

"Do you mean it, Juha?" the boys said eagerly. "Are you sure?"

"Why, of course I'm sure," said Juha. He felt well pleased with his cleverness as he watched the boys run off in the direction of the big house—where, in fact, as Juha perfectly well knew, no wedding was even thought of, much less taking place.

Juha had just begun to nod again when he was waked by another group of boys running by, calling to all the children in the market as they passed. "Candy!" they called. "Come on, run, candy for everyone at the wedding!" He smiled to himself and closed his eyes again.

In a moment there were more running feet passing him, more children and adults, too. Juha watched them in surprise. "Juha," one of the men called to him. "Get up and come to the wedding, lazy one. Don't you know there is a wedding in the big house at the end of the village, and they have fine refreshments for everyone?"

"How do you know?" asked Juha, sitting up.

"Why, everybody says so," the man said. "The whole town is talking about it."

Juha rubbed his eyes and got up. He stood for a moment, puzzled. Then, thinking that he had better get to the wedding before all the refreshments were eaten up, he began to run after the others.

A GUEST FOR HALIL

TURKEY: The "hodja," which means wise man, teacher or judge, is a popular hero of Middle Eastern stories, and dozens of tales are told about his ingenuity and wit. This one is by Alice Geer Kelsey.

"Hurry! You will be late for the banquet at Halil's house!" One person after another called this advice to Nasr-ed-Din Hodja as he jogged home from a day's work in his vineyard.

"They are right," the Hodja finally admitted. The sun was almost touching the horizon. "I will be late for the dinner, unless I go now— just as I am."

He turned his reluctant donkey's head about and was soon at Halil's house. He tied his donkey in Halil's courtyard and walked confidently into the house, where the feast was soon to begin. Always sure of a welcome, he spread his smiles and his jokes to right and to left. He was so happy talking that he did not notice for some time a very strange thing. He was talking to backs instead of to faces. Not a single man was listening to him! Soon an even stranger thing happened. When the soup was brought in, Halil ushered other men to seats at the low table, but he had no word for Nasr-ed-Din Hodja.

The Hodja cleared his throat noisily. Halil did not notice. He coughed loudly. Halil paid no attention.

"Oh, Halil Effendi!" called Nasr-ed-Din Hodja cheerily. "I noticed a fine crop of fruit in your vineyard today."

Halil, busy with his well-dressed guests, did not hear.

"Oh, Halil Effendi!" The Hodja's voice was even louder this time. "Your smallest grapes are twice as big as the best in my vineyard."

Still Halil seemed unable to hear or to see the one guest who stood alone in his shabby, dirty working clothes.

The Hodja looked thoughtfully at the other guests. Each man was scrubbed till he glistened. Each man was wearing his best clothes. Then the Hodja looked at his own brown hands, caked with the honest dirt of the vineyards. He looked at his own clothes with their patches upon patches, and with the day's new holes which the patient Fatima would mend that night.

Very quietly, Nasr-ed-Din Hodja slipped out of the door, untied his willing donkey and jogged home.

"Hot water, Fatima!" he ordered. "Soap, Fatima! My new shoes! My best turban! My new coat!"

Fatima bustled and fluttered about. Soon Nasr-ed-Din Hodja looked like a new man. He preened himself before the admiring Fatima, who had not seen her husband so completely well dressed in years. He strutted out of the house. Little boys spoke to him respectfully as he swaggered back along the street to Halil's house. Women peered from behind their veils at the grand gentleman who walked with such an air.

A bowing servant ushered him into the banquet room at Halil's house. A beaming Halil hurried to meet him and escort him to the best seat in the room. Men smiled and nodded. Halil heaped his plate with goodies. Questions and stories were directed toward Nasr-ed-Din Hodja.

When he felt that all eyes were upon him, the Hodja picked up the choicest piece of meat on his plate. He did not raise it tò his lips. Instead, he opened his coat and placed it in a pocket which was hidden inside.

"Eat, coat, eat!" said the Hodja.

A handful of pilaf, a square of cheese, a pickle, and a fig followed the meat into the coat.

"Eat, coat, eat!" said the Hodja as he put in each tidbit. The guests stopped eating to watch the Hodja feed his coat.

Finally, Halil could hold in no longer. "Tell me, Hodja Effendi, what you mean by telling your coat to eat."

"Why, surely, you wish the coat to eat." The Hodja raised innocent eyes to Halil. "When I came in my old clothes, there was no place at the table for me. When I come in my new clothes, nothing is too good for me. That shows it was the coat, not me, that you invited to your banquet."

THE

A VERY LONG TIME AGO, somewhere in that far away land of Tibet, away up so high that it seems a little nearer to the sky than any other land, in one corner was a country governed by a very just man. He was noted in all parts of the dominion for his fair judgment in all cases. In the city where this good king lived and had his home, dwelt two poor men. Both were very good, did the very best they could every day, and each had an old mother to support.

One day one of the men started to a village high up in the mountains carrying a jar of oil, selling it as he went. Walking along, he grew very tired and set his jar of oil on a rock by the roadside while he sat down to rest a while. As he sat there, his neighbor came down the mountain driving his donkey in front of him. There were two big loads of wood, stacked one on each side of the little donkey, which almost covered him. He didn't happen to see the jar, so came too near and knocked it off, breaking it, and spilling all the oil.

The man who owned the oil was very angry indeed, and the man who owned the donkey said it wasn't he who had done the damage, but the donkey. So they quarreled and quarreled and kept on quarreling. The man who owned the oil said he couldn't afford to lose it, as it was all he had in the world to sell for food for his mother and himself, and it couldn't have been his fault the jar was broken.

They both went to the king who questioned them very carefully about the matter and finally said he couldn't see that either one was to blame. They were both good men, took good care of their old mothers and were honest in all their dealings, and so far as he could see no one was at fault but the donkey and the rock, and he would judge them.

DONKEY AND THE ROCK

TIBET: Judges, both good and bad, appear in folk tales almost as often as brave heroes do. Here is a story about two odd defendants and a judgment that is both wise and tricky.

So the little donkey was led into prison with chains around his legs and his neck, while five of the king's men were sent out for the rock. The king ordered it wrapped with chains and tied outside the prison door to a post.

By this time the news of this strange case and the queer doings of the king had spread throughout the city. When the people heard their great king was having a trial about a donkey and a rock they thought he had surely gone mad. The next morning the king announced, by his runners through the city, that the case would be tried. The idea that a donkey and a rock could have a trial in court was more than the people could understand, but early next day everybody in the city was at the courtyard to see the result of the trial.

When the time arrived the judge came, took his seat, instructed the doorkeepers to shut and lock all the gates, thus locking in everybody, and then proceeded to pronounce his judgment on the case.

"As you very well know, there is no law by which a donkey and a rock can be judged. Why have you all come to see so absurd a thing? Now, because of your curiosity in the matter, every one of you shall pay a half-cent before he gets out."

The people, looking much ashamed, and glad to get out, handed over this bit of money and slipped through the gate. The cash taken in this way was given to the man who had lost his oil, so he was happy, the debt was paid, and the court closed.

BASTIANELO

ITALY, SAN MARINO: This story, by T. F. Crane, is an Italian favorite, but it is told in many other countries, too.

ONCE UPON A TIME there was a husband and wife who had a son. This son grew up and said to his mother one day, "Do you know, Mother, I would like to marry!"

"Very well, marry. Whom do you want to take?"

"I want the gardener's daughter," he answered.

"She's a good girl," the mother said. "Take her. I am willing."

So the son went and asked for the girl, and her parents gave her to him. They were married, and when they were in the midst of the wedding dinner, the wine gave out.

Anxious to show what a good housekeeper she was, the bride hopped up and said, "I will go and get some more wine." She took the bottles and went to the cellar. As she was turning the cock of the wine cask, she began to think,

"Suppose I should have a son, and we should call him Bastianelo, and he should die. Oh, how grieved I should be! Oh, how grieved I should be!" And thereupon she began to weep and weep, and meanwhile the wine was running all over the cellar.

When the others saw the bride did not return with the wine, the mother said, "I will go and see what the matter is." So she went into the cellar and saw the bride with a bottle in her hand, weeping, while the wine was running all over the cellar.

"What is the matter with you that you weep so?" asked the mother.

"Ah, my mother, I was thinking that if I had a son and should name him Bastianelo and he should die, oh, how I should grieve! Oh, how I should grieve!"

The mother, too, began to weep and weep,

and meanwhile the wine was running all over the cellar.

When the people at the table saw that no one brought the wine, the bride's father said, "I will go and see what is the matter. Certainly something has happened to the bride." He went and saw the whole cellar full of wine, and the mother and bride weeping. "What is the matter?" he said. "Has anything happened to you?"

"No," said the bride, "but I was thinking that if I had a son and should call him Bastianelo and he should die, oh, how I should grieve! Oh, how I should grieve!" Then the father, too, began to weep and all three wept, and meanwhile the wine was running all over the cellar.

When the groom saw that neither the bride nor the mother nor the father came back, he said, "Now I will go and see what the matter is, that no one returns." He went down the steps and saw the wine running all over the cellar. He hastened to shut off the cock and then asked, "What is the matter that you are all weeping and have let the wine run all over the cellar?"

Then the bride said, "I was thinking that if I had a son and called him Bastianelo and he should die, oh, how I should grieve! Oh, how I should grieve!"

"You stupid fools!" the groom said, "are you weeping at this, and letting the wine run into the cellar? Have you nothing else to think of? It shall never be said that I remained here with you! I will roam about the world and, until I find three fools greater than you, I will not return home."

He had a bread-cake made, took a bottle of wine, a sausage, and some linen, and made a bundle, which he put on a stick and carried over his shoulder. He journeyed and journeyed, and began to despair of finding a fool greater than his wife. He thought of turning back, but at that moment, he saw a man in his shirt sleeves at a well, all wet with perspiration and water.

"What are you doing, sir, that you are so covered with water and in such a sweat?"

"Oh, let me alone," the man answered. "For I have been here a long time drawing water to fill this pail and I cannot fill it."

"What are you drawing the water in?" the groom asked.

"In a sieve," the man said.

"What are you thinking about, drawing water in a sieve? Just wait." The groom went to a house nearby and borrowed a bucket with which he promptly filled the pail.

"Thank you, good sir," said the man. "Heaven knows how long I should have had to remain here!"

"Here is one who is a greater fool than my wife," thought the groom.

He continued his journey and after a time he saw a man in his shirt who was jumping down from a tree. As he drew near, he saw a woman under the tree holding a pair of breeches. He asked them what they were doing, and they said they had been there a long time and that the man wanted to try on those breeches, but did not know how to get into them.

"I have jumped and jumped until I am tired out," said the man. "And I cannot imagine how to get into these breeches."

"No wonder," said the groom. "You will never get into them that way. Come down and lean against the tree." Then he picked up the man's legs and put them one by one into the breeches. After he had pulled the breeches up, he said, "Is that right?"

"Very good, bless you, for if it had not been for you, heaven knows how long I should have had to jump."

The groom said to himself, "Now I have seen two greater fools than my wife." Then he went on his way, shaking his head in astonishment.

As he approached a city, he heard a great noise. When he drew near, he asked what it was and was told that it was a marriage and that it was the custom in that city for brides to enter the city gate on horseback. On this occasion, there was a great discussion between the husband and the owner of the horse, for the bride was tall and the horse high and they could not get through the gate. They argued that they must either cut off the bride's head or the horse's legs. The husband did not wish his bride's head cut off, and the owner did not wish his horse's legs cut off — hence the disturbance.

Then the groom said, "Just wait." He went up to the bride and gave her a slap that made her lower her head, and then he gave the horse a kick and so they passed through the gate and entered the city.

The husband and the owner of the horse asked the groom how they could reward him, for he had saved the husband his bride and the owner his horse. He answered that he did not wish anything and said to himself, "Two and one make three! That is enough. Now I shall go home."

He hurried home and said to his wife, "Here I am, my wife. I have seen three greater fools than you. Now let us remain in peace and think about nothing else." They renewed the wedding and always remained in peace. After a time, the wife had a son whom they named Bastianelo, and Bastianelo did not die, but still lives with his father and mother.

In other versions, the stupidities are different, but the husband always finds that the world is full of silly people and decides that he might as well return to his silly wife.

PIPILO

ALBANIA: This story comes from an Albanian-English reader. It was written by an Albanian boy who had heard it from his grandparents.

ONCE UPON A TIME in a small village in Albania, there lived three brothers. The youngest and tallest of the three was named Pipilo. Although they were hard-working young men, they were often hungry, for an Ogress who lived in their quarter of the village, stole everything she could lay her hands on. The villagers were afraid to oppose her, because if she could not find chickens or sheep to steal, she would snatch a child for her dinner. The villagers got so they quivered at the sound of her voice, and mothers made children hide under the beds when the Ogress walked abroad.

Pipilo, who was as brave as he was tall, decided to get revenge on the Ogress. Working at night while she slept, he dug a tunnel. It started at his house and came out inside the Ogress' walled courtyard, where he carefully covered the opening with branches and leaves.

The first night he stole into the courtyard, he saw her shepherd and said to him, "Come with me, shepherd. I will free you from the power of the Ogress."

The shepherd did not heed his words, but at once called out, "Pipilo is trying to carry me off!" Pipilo quickly dived back into the mouth of the tunnel and, when the Ogress stormed out of her house, he was safely hidden.

"Where are you hiding Pipilo, fellow?" the Ogress demanded of the shepherd. When he could not tell her, she beat him unmercifully.

The second night, Pipilo returned and repeated the same words to the shepherd. This time, the shepherd, remembering the beating of the night before, gladly came with Pipilo, herding the sheep before him down the tunnel. When the Ogress woke the next morning, she saw her sheep and shepherd were missing.

"Oh, Pipilo! Oh, Pipilo!" she screamed.

"Sheep and shepherd and all you've taken from me."

After two or three nights, Pipilo went again to the Ogress' house and called to her doves, throwing down grain for them. The doves, however, did not heed the grain, but trembled with

fear and cried out, "Pipilo is trying to carry us off!"

Pipilo again hid in the tunnel, and when the Ogress appeared, she was unable to find him.

"Where is Pipilo hiding?" she demanded of the doves angrily, and when they could not tell her, she hit them with a stick.

The next night, Pipilo returned and threw more grain for the doves. This time they followed him into the tunnel.

After keeping quiet for some nights, Pipilo went through the tunnel again to lure away the Ogress' horse. He threw raisins and chickpeas to it to persuade it. The horse, however, neighed loudly and said, "Pipilo is trying to carry me off!"

When the Ogress appeared this time, she said, "Yes, yes! Pipilo has got into the habit of carrying off my livestock." Then she beat the horse saying, "What do I want with you when my sheep and doves are gone? You go, too, with Pipilo."

So the next night, Pipilo came and led the horse through the tunnel.

After two or three months, Pipilo dressed himself like a carpenter and went to the Ogress' forest to saw some planks. As soon as the Ogress saw him, she said, "Hi! you there, what do you want in my forest?"

"I've come to saw some planks," said Pipilo in a disguised voice. "An evil man named Pipilo has just died and I need planks for his coffin."

The Ogress was delighted. "Oh, take all the planks you want," she said. "Here, let me help. We'll make the coffin together. Pipilo was indeed an evil man. He stole my sheep and shepherd from me. He took my doves from me. And he even led my horse away."

After they had made the coffin, Pipilo said to the Ogress, "Hop in a moment to see if the coffin is long enough. Pipilo's very tall, you know, just about your size."

"Yes, yes," said the Ogress. "He is very tall," and she hopped into the coffin.

Quickly Pipilo nailed down the lid and carried the coffin to his own house where his brothers had built a great fire. They threw the coffin, Ogress and all, into the blaze and burned her up.

And ever since then, Pipilo and his brothers and the rest of the village have been happy and prosperous.

THE CONCEITED SPIDER

NIGERIA: It is no accident that so many stories are told about Anansi. By W. H. Barker and C. Sinclair.

IN THE OLDEN DAYS, all the stories men told were stories of Nyankupon, the chief of the Gods. Anansi the Spider, who was very conceited, wanted all the stories to be told about

him. So one day he went to Nyankupon and asked that, in the future, all tales told by men might be Anansi stories instead of Nyankupon stories.

Nyankupon agreed, on one condition. He told Anansi the Spider that he must bring him three things: the first was a jar full of live bees, the second was a boa-constrictor, and the third was a tiger. Anansi gave his promise.

He took an earthen jar and set out for a place where he knew there were numbers of bees. When he came in sight of the bees, he began saying to himself, "They will not be able to fill this jar." "Yes, they will be able." "No, they will not be able."

Finally the bees came up to him and said, "What are you talking about, Mr. Anansi?"

He then explained to them that Nyankupon and he had had a great dispute. Nyankupon had said the bees could not fly into the jar. Anansi had said they could. The bees immediately declared that, of course, they could fly into the jar. And they did. As soon as they were safely inside, Anansi sealed up the jar and sent it to Nyankupon.

Next day, he took a long stick and set out in search of a boa-constrictor. When he arrived at the place where one lived, he began speaking to himself again. "He will be just as long as this stick." "No, he will not be as long as this." "Yes, he will be as long as this."

He repeated these words several times, until the boa-constrictor came out and asked him what was the matter.

"Oh, we have been having a dispute in Nyankupon's town about you," said Anansi. "Nyankupon's people say you are not as long as this stick. I say you are. Would you please let me measure you by it?"

The boa innocently laid himself out straight, and Spider lost no time in tying him on to the stick from end to end. Then, when the boa was helpless, he sent him to Nyankupon.

The third day, he took some gum and glued his eye shut. He then set out for a den where he knew a tiger lived. As he approached the place, he began to shout and sing so loudly that the tiger came out to see what was the matter.

"Can you not see?" said Anansi. "My eyelids are glued together and now I can see such wonderful things that I must sing about them."

"Glue my eyelids," said the tiger, "so that I, too, may see these amazing sights."

Anansi immediately did so, and having made the tiger helpless, he led him straight to Nyankupon's house. Nyankupon was astonished at Anansi's cleverness in accomplishing the three tasks.

"From now on," Nyankupon said, "you have my permission to call all the old tales Anansi tales."

And that is why, in Nyankupon's country, all the stories are Anansi's.

THE SILLY FELLOW WHO SOLD HIS BEARD

GYPSY: Gypsies, who speak a language called Romany, are thought to have come originally from India. They now live in many countries. This story is told by Swedish gypsies, and it starts with the standard phrase that gypsy storytellers use to signal the beginning of a story. By M. A. Jagendorf and C. H. Tillhagen.

IF IT HADN'T HAPPENED, it wouldn't be told.

Once there were two merchants who were good friends. One was smart and one was silly; the smart one was clean-shaven, like a young boy, and the other had a long, thick beard. Take my word for it, it was a very handsome beard.

One day they were sitting together talking of this and that. Said the one who had no beard:

"Little brother, would you like to sell me your beard?"

The one with the beard answered: "Why not, if you'll pay me a good price?"

"I'll give you whatever you ask for that fine beard of yours."

"I'll let you name the price, good friend. I know you'll be fair," said the one with the beard.

"Fine. I'll give you a good sum, but on one condition. I want the beard to keep on growing on *your* face, but *I* will take care of it—how it is to grow, how it is to be combed, what perfume is to be put on it, and how it should be cut. Everything will have to be done as I like it. You won't have the right to say anything about it. That beard will be all mine. If anyone says to you, 'What a beautiful beard!' you'll have to answer quickly, 'Sorry, my good man, it's not my beard, it belongs to so-and-so.' That's what you'll have to say."

The man with the beard had no objection to that.

"Sure, friend," he said. "You can keep looking after my beard—I mean your beard. It will be cheaper for me!"

So they wrote out a contract, and the merchant who was clean-shaven paid a good sum to the other.

Mischtó! Fine and dandy. From that day on the clean-shaven man was very particular about taking care of the beard he had bought on his friend's face and he stopped at nothing to show it. Whenever he felt like it or thought of it, which was many a time during a day, he came to tend to the beard his merchant friend had on his chin. It made no difference to him whether his friend had company or whether he was asleep. And sometimes he wasn't too gentle about the beard, either. He'd pull it and tug it. Sometimes he'd cut it to a point, sometimes in

squares or zigzag. One day he'd smear sweet-scented oil over it, and the next, he'd pour on it heaven knows what.

If the poor sufferer complained, it was like talking to the wind. His crying and wailing just struck a stone wall.

"Listen, friend; listen, you there! Are you out of your mind? You're acting like a crazy man. Leave my beard in peace."

"Well, here is something," the one who had bought the beard cried. "Grumbling and kicking! Maybe you'd like to break your contract! You'll get into trouble if you do. The law is on my side. Just keep calm. That beard belongs to me, and I have the right to do with it as I wish."

And then he went at that beard hammer and nails. He tugged it and pulled it until the poor merchant screamed to heaven.

So time went by while the one who bought the beard kept tearing and teasing the beard of the one who had it on his chin. In the end the poor sufferer couldn't stand it any longer.

"Little brother, good friend, I want to buy back my beard. For the love of our good God, let me have my beard again. You are making my life worse than if I lived with the Devil."

"Don't talk foolishly. I am very happy with my beard on your face. It's a nice beard; it's thick and glossy. Look how strong the roots of the hair are," he said as he began to pull it. "I want to keep it. Maybe later on we'll see what can be done."

And so he kept on taking care of the beard in his own way and as he felt like it. In the end it was too much for the bearded merchant.

"I want to buy my beard back," he cried. "Little brother, I want my beard, you are driving me crazy. Give it back to me and I'll pay you any price."

"How much do you offer?"

"I'll give you twice as much as you paid me."

"Twice as much for this fine, thick, glossy beard! Just feel it," and he got hold of it. "You'll have to go higher, brother."

"Ow! Let go! Name any price. I'll give you whatever you ask."

"That's talking! Give me four times as much as I gave you, and you'll pay just right for your beard—and your foolishness!"

So the bearded merchant paid the other. And then he quickly went to the barber and had his beard shaved off.

THE RAM AND THE LION'S SON

UNION OF SOUTH AFRICA: The Bushmen of South Africa tell this particular story, but animal stories much like it turn up in other countries, too.

THE LION's son had become old enough to hunt for himself and not to wait upon the pleasure of his father and mother. One day, when he was returning home from hunting by himself, he came upon the home of a Ram. Now this young Lion had never before seen a Ram and, therefore, approached him timidly.

"Good day, friend," he said. "And what may your name be?"

The Ram was terrified, for the Lion's son, though young, was large and strong, with mighty claws and teeth, and his muscles rippled slickly under his yellow hide. But the Ram was too clever to let the young Lion know of his feelings, so he struck his chest with his forefoot and said in his gruffest, most menacing voice, "I am a Ram. Who are you?"

22

"A Lion," the young one whispered, frightened out of his wits by the Ram's voice and actions. "Good-bye friend!" And he ran home as fast as he could.

When the young Lion was almost home, he met his friend, the Jackal. "Slow down, friend," the Jackal said soothingly, standing squarely in his path. "From what do you flee in such a panic?"

"Oh, friend Jackal," the Lion's son gasped, panting and puffing, "I am half dead with fright, for I have just seen the most dreadful creature, the like of which I've never seen before. He looked as though he would attack me with his huge, thick head and, when I asked his name, he thumped his chest and growled, 'I am a Ram!'"

"A Ram!" cried the Jackal. "Do you mean to say you went off and left a delicious meal like that just standing there? For goodness' sake, where are your brains? Come, we will go back together and eat it."

"Oh, no, friend Jackal, I couldn't," moaned the Lion's son. "From the looks of this fierce beast, I think we may be the ones who will be eaten."

"Nonsense!" said the Jackal. "Come, we will tie ourselves together with this leather thong.

Then you will know I will always stay with you."

"Well, if you really think it's all right," said the Lion's son. "But I am no less frightened to know he will eat us both instead of only myself."

They started off for the home of the Ram, and the Ram, who was out looking for the tenderest greens for supper, saw them coming over the crest of the hill. He whirled and ran to his wife, calling, "Wife! Wife! I fear this is the last day of our lives, for the Lion is coming back, and this time he has brought a Jackal with him! What shall we do?"

"Don't be afraid," said his wife. "Take the child in your arms and, when you see them coming near, pinch it to make it cry as if it were hungry. I'll do the rest."

The Ram did as his wife said, and went out with the child in his arms toward the approaching companions. When the Lion's son saw the Ram, his legs began to go weak and he shivered all over with fright. He tried to turn back, but the leather thong held him fast to the Jackal, who continued to walk toward the Ram saying, "Come on, friend, there's nothing to fear!"

When the Lion's son and the Jackal were near, the Ram pinched his child and the child bellowed in anger and pain. The wife came running out, saw the approaching companions and called above the uproar, "You have done well, friend Jackal, to have brought us such a fine supper as Lion meat. And just in time, too. Hear how the child cries for food!"

On hearing these dreadful words, the Lion's son turned tail and set off the way he had come, dragging the Jackal after him. There was no time in his terrified flight to stop and let the Jackal loose, even though he begged and pleaded. He dragged the howling Jackal over hill and valley, through bushes and over rocks. And he never stopped to look behind him until he and the half-dead Jackal came to the home of his father.

But the Ram and his wife comforted their offended child, and they all spent the rest of the day eating the most delicious greens for supper.

THE TIGER, THE BRAHMAN, AND THE JACKAL

INDIA, BHUTAN, NEPAL: In this version of a very old story the cunning hero is a jackal. By Joseph Jacobs.

O NCE UPON A TIME, a tiger was caught in a trap. He tried in vain to get out through the bars, and rolled and bit with rage and grief when he failed.

By chance a poor Brahman came by.

"Let me out of this cage, oh, pious one!" cried the tiger.

"Nay, my friend," replied the Brahman mildly, "you would probably eat me if I did."

"Not at all!" swore the tiger with many oaths; "on the contrary, I should be forever grateful, and serve you as a slave!"

Now when the tiger sobbed and sighed and wept and swore, the pious Brahman's heart softened, and at last he consented to open the door of the cage. Out popped the tiger, and, seizing the poor man, cried, "What a fool you are! What is to prevent my eating you now, for after being cooped up so long I am just terribly hungry!"

In vain the Brahman pleaded for his life; the most he could gain was a promise to abide by the decision of the first three things he chose to question as to the justice of the tiger's action.

So the Brahman first asked a pipal tree what it thought of the matter, but the pipal tree replied coldly: "What have you to complain about? Don't I give shade and shelter to every one who passes by, and don't they in return tear down my branches to feed their cattle? Don't whimper—be a man!"

Then the Brahman, sad at heart, went farther afield till he saw a buffalo turning a well-wheel;

24

but he fared no better from it, for it answered; "You are a fool to expect gratitude! Look at me! Whilst I gave milk they fed me on cotton-seed and oil-cake, but now I am dry they yoke me here, and give me refuse as fodder!"

The Brahman, still more sad, asked the road to give him its opinion.

"My dear sir," said the road, "how foolish you are to expect anything else! Here am I, useful to everybody, yet all, rich and poor, great and small, trample on me as they go past, giving me nothing but the ashes of their pipes and the husks of their grain!"

On this the Brahman turned back sorrowfully, and on the way he met a jackal, who called out: "Why, what's the matter, Mr. Brahman? You look as miserable as a fish out of water!"

The Brahman told him all that had occurred. "How very confusing!" said the jackal, when the recital was ended; "would you mind telling me over again, for everything has got so mixed up?"

The Brahman told it all over again, but the jackal shook his head in a distracted sort of way, and still could not understand.

"It's very odd," said he, sadly, "but it all seems to go in at one ear and out at the other! I will go to the place where it all happened, and then perhaps I shall be able to give a judgment."

So they returned to the cage, by which the tiger was waiting for the Brahman, and sharpening his teeth and claws.

"You've been away a long time!" growled the savage beast, "but now let us begin our dinner."

"*Our* dinner!" thought the wretched Brahman, as his knees knocked together with fright; "what a remarkably delicate way of putting it!"

"Give me five minutes, my lord!" he pleaded, "in order that I may explain matters to the jackal here, who is somewhat slow in his wits."

The tiger consented, and the Brahman began the whole story over again, not missing a single detail, and spinning as long a yarn as possible.

"Oh, my poor brain! oh, my poor brain!" cried the jackal, wringing his paws. "Let me see! how did it all begin? You were in the cage, and the tiger came walking by—"

"Pooh," interrupted the tiger, "what a fool you are! *I* was in the cage."

"Of course!" cried the jackal, pretending to tremble with fright; "yes! I was in the cage—no I wasn't—dear! dear! where are my wits? Let me see—the tiger was in the Brahman, and the cage came walking by—no, that's not it, either! Well, don't mind me, but begin your dinner, for I shall never understand!"

"Yes, you shall!" returned the tiger, in a rage at the jackal's stupidity; "I'll *make* you understand! Look here—I am the tiger—"

"Yes, my lord!"

"And that is the Brahman—"

"Yes, my lord!"

"And that is the cage—"

"Yes, my lord!"

"And I was in the cage—do you understand?"

"Yes—no—Please, my lord—"

"Well?" cried the tiger impatiently.

"Please, my lord!—how did you get in?"

"How!—why in the usual way, of course!"

"Oh, dear me!—my head is beginning to whirl again. Please don't be angry, my lord, but what is the usual way?"

At this the tiger lost patience, and, jumping into the cage, cried: "This way! Now do you understand how it was?"

"Perfectly!" grinned the jackal, as he dexterously shut the door, "and if you will permit me to say so, I think matters will remain as they were!"

THE BRAHMAN'S DREAM

INDIA, BHUTAN, NEPAL: Variations of this story from the *Panchatantra* a two-thousand-year-old Indian classic, are told in dozens of languages.

I N A CERTAIN TOWN lived a Brahman named Seedy, who got some barley-meal by begging, ate a portion, and filled a jar with the remainder. This jar he hung on a peg one night, placed his cot beneath it, and fixing his gaze on the jar, fell into a hypnotic reverie.

"Well, here is a jar full of barley-meal," he thought. "Now, if famine comes, a hundred rupees will come out of it. With that sum I will get two she-goats. Every six months they will bear two more she-goats. After goats, cows. When the cows calve, I will sell the calves. After cows, buffaloes; after buffaloes, mares. From the mares I shall get plenty of horses. The sale of these will mean plenty of gold. The gold will buy a great house with an inner court. Then someone will come to my house and offer his lovely daughter with a dowry. She will bear a son whom I shall name Moon-Lord. When he is old enough to ride on my knee, I will take a book, sit on the stable roof, and think. Just then Moon-Lord will see me, will jump from his mother's lap in his eagerness to ride on my knee, and will go too near the horses. Then I shall get angry and tell my wife to take the boy. But she will be busy with her chores and will not pay attention to what I say. Then I will get up and kick her."

In his daydream he let fly such a kick that he smashed the jar. And the barley-meal which it contained turned him white all over.

26

THE VEGETABLE TREE

MAYAN: The Mayans liked to tell how things began. An old story retold by Dorothy Rhoads.

I HAD THE TALE from my mother, who heard it from her mother. And she, no doubt, had heard the tale from her own mother, and so back through the centuries.

It was in the very beginning of the world. . . . There were no coconut trees and no mango trees or orange trees or bananas as there are today. And there were no bean plants or squash or chili or cassava. All the vegetables and all the fruits in the world (except corn) grew on one enormous tree which stood in the exact center of the world. And every day the animals came to the tree and ate from it. But man did not know the tree existed.

Who the first man was who found the tree, no one knows. Long ago his name was forgotten. But the man came to the tree, and he saw the vegetables and fruits that drooped heavily from the branches. And he decided to chop down the tree and plant the seed.

All day the man chopped and cut at the tree trunk with his machete. And at the end of the day he was weary, and he went to sleep. And in the morning he awoke. And there was no trace in the tree of the work he had done the day before.

All the second day the man chopped at the tree, and he cut into the trunk a few inches. And when the sun went down he was weary, and he went to sleep. And on the next day when he arose, there was no trace in the tree trunk where the man had worked the day before.

And the man brought one of his friends. And the two men cut and chopped at the base of the tree with their machetes. And they cut away several inches. And when the darkness fell they were weary, and they went to sleep. But when they awoke in the morning, there was no mark or cut in the trunk of the tree.

And the two men called other men. And they chopped and cut at the tree, and by the end of the day the men had cut halfway through the tree trunk. And they were weary, and they went to sleep. And in the morning there was no trace of their work of the day before.

And the whole village set to work to chop down the tree, and they cut and chopped all the day. And when the darkness fell, only a small piece of the tree trunk remained to be cut. And the men were weary from their work. And they lay down and went to sleep. And in the morning there was no trace of the cutting and chopping of the day before.

Then one of the men suggested wisely:

"Let us chop again at the tree. And if it happens that we do not cut through the trunk, let us remain awake and see what takes place during the night."

And all day the men cut and chopped at the tree. And when darkness fell they were weary. And they remained awake.

And in the darkness of the night the animals of the bush gathered about the tree. The jaguar was there, and the deer; and the fox and wild pig and ocelot and serpent and tepizcuintle and the armadillo. Every animal and every bird and every crawling thing of the bush gathered about the tree. And the animals began to work. They took up from around the base of the tree the chips that the men had cut out the day before, and they replaced the chips in the trunk of the tree. They worked all night, each animal and crawling thing and bird, replacing the chips. And before the light returned they had replaced all the chips, and the tree was whole.

All the next day the men worked chopping and cutting at the tree. And when the evening came there was only a small bit of the tree trunk that remained to be cut. And the men were weary, but they did not stop. They cut and chopped at the tree in the darkness, and the tree trunk was cut through. And the tree fell. And the men gathered the fruit and hurried away to plant the seed.

Today there are coconut trees and mango trees and orange trees and bananas. And there are beans and squash and chili and cassava. Each fruit and each vegetable grows on its own plant and on its own tree.

I heard the tale from my mother, who had it from her mother. And her mother had had it from her own mother back and back through the centuries.

It was in the very beginning of the world. . . .

THE CANDLE IN THE DARKNESS

ETHIOPIA, SUDAN, SOMALIA: This gentle, pleasant joke is a favorite in North Africa. Adapted from a story by Leslie W. Leavitt.

ON A COLD EVENING, Yasu and several of his friends were gathered about the fire in Yasu's house, toasting themselves and telling stories. The wind whistled around the corner of the house and spatters of snow could be heard against the windows. But inside the men were comfortable and warm.

Soon each man's story telling turned upon himself, and the friends were vying with one another with tales to prove their bravery and strength. As they went on, they became boastful, not about what they had done, but about what they could do if the occasion arose. Finally, Yasu, having listened to the boasts of the others politely, said, "I, too, am exceedingly strong. And I have great courage and fortitude."

His friend, Mikael, scoffed, for Yasu was not a powerful or outstandingly bold man. "What can you do," he said, "that would show you are particularly fearless?"

"Well, let me see," said Yasu. "Can any of you think of a deed I could perform now?"

None of his friends could.

"Nevertheless," said Yasu, "since Mikael seems to doubt my courage, I must prove it. Will this convince you, Mikael? I will stay out all night in the snow with no fire to give me heat."

"Yes, my friend," said Mikael, "it would convince me. But I have no desire to see you freeze to death to prove your point."

Ali joined Mikael in protesting, "Don't do it, Yasu. The night is becoming colder every minute and the snow falls more thickly. You will freeze with no fire."

"Not I," said Yasu. "I am very strong. I know I can do it, and I intend to prove it to all of you this very night."

"Please, Yasu," said Mikael, "I do not want to be responsible for the death of my friend."

"You will not be, Mikael. I will stand out in the cold all night. I will have no fire for warmth, and I will come in when the sun rises, as healthy as I ever was. If I do not succeed—and I have no doubt that I will—I shall . . . shall give you all a big dinner here at my house."

"All right, then," said Yasu's friends, "since you insist on being stubborn, we will admit that you have great strength and great courage if you can stay all night in the cold. But remember, you cannot have any kind of fire to warm you, and you cannot go indoors, or we will demand the dinner in payment."

Yasu's friends left then, to go to their own houses and their warm beds. Yasu went out into the snow. At first, the air felt like ice and he shivered. After a few minutes, he became more accustomed to the cold and did not mind it as much. Then he settled down to wait out the night. He walked slowly up and down watching the lights in the houses go out. Soon there was no light to be seen, only darkness and the cold wet snow falling about him and melting on his shoulders and back. The town was silent. A great loneliness came over him, and he wished he could see the stars, but snow clouds covered the sky.

He realized his fingers were icy. He thrust them into his sleeves for warmth and walked more briskly to warm his legs and feet. Back and forth, back and forth, across the open square he paced. The hours must be passing, he thought, but how slowly they went! There was no sign of light in the eastern sky—only cold, gray darkness. Yasu's hands and feet grew numb. The snow had become too deep to walk through easily, so he stood in one place, stamping off the minutes. He removed his hands from his sleeves and rubbed his legs until they tingled, then covered his hands again.

How unfriendly the night was, and how dreadfully dark! A strong urge came over him

to lie down where he was and sleep, but he knew he must keep moving or he would surely freeze to death. The thought frightened him and he started walking again, kicking his way through the snow, stumbling and slipping. Then he stopped. Far off, in a window of one of the village houses, a candle had been lighted. He could barely see its tiny glow through the falling snow. But it burned steadfastly—warm and somehow friendly. The person who had lit the candle hadn't even known he was there, but the little flame was like a magic sign that he was not all alone in the dark. There were other people near him and awake.

Now he was no longer afraid. He watched the candle every minute, and its light helped him to fight off sleep. Its friendliness told him that he could last out the night. Four o'clock . . . five o'clock . . . a glimmer of light showed in the eastern sky. The light grew brighter and the candle went out, but by now it was almost time for sunrise. With a surge of triumph, Yasu knew he had succeeded!

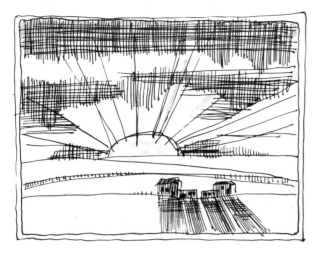

With the first blaze of the sun over the horizon, Yasu turned and plodded back to his house on feet that felt nothing. It seemed he would never be warm again, but when he reached his comfortable house and stirred up the embers of his fire, a glow came over him. It was partly the warmth of his hearth, but it was also the knowledge that he had proved his courage and strength to his doubting friends.

At about ten o'clock, there was a knock on Yasu's door and his companions of the night before came in. "Did you manage to stay out all night, Yasu?" Mikael said.

"Yes, I stayed out until the sun rose," said Yasu.

"And you had no fire to keep you warm?"

"No, not the smallest fire."

"How did you ever do it?" asked Ali wonderingly. "Wasn't it terribly hard?"

"It certainly was," said Yasu. "I am very strong and I am very brave, but I confess there was a time when I thought I might have to give up. But then someone lit a candle in a window far across the village. It was amazing what encouragement the sight of that little flame gave me. . . ."

"Did you say a candle, Yasu?" Mikael broke in.

"Yes, a candle."

"Ah, but a candle gives out heat. And you said you would stay out all night with no heat of any kind. You did not do what you said you would do."

Yasu snorted. "How can a candle all the way

over on the other side of the village warm someone who is standing in the square?"

"You can argue if you like, Yasu. But a candle gives out heat. You may have felt very little, but you did get some heat from it. You must give us that dinner as you promised."

Yasu turned to the others for support, but they laughed and said, "He's right. You had the heat of the candle. We want the dinner you owe us. We want it tonight."

Yasu argued and protested, but none of his friends would listen. Finally he said sadly, "All right. Come for dinner when the sun goes down."

When the door had closed behind his friends, Yasu sat down to think. He thought and thought. . . .

Just as the sun was going down, all the men

arrived at Yasu's house laughing and talking. "Here we are, Yasu," they shouted to him as they took seats around the room. "Is the dinner ready?"

"No," Yasu called from the next room, "not yet. But please sit down."

They sat back comfortably, chatting with one another, and waited. From time to time they could hear Yasu moving about in the next room, but, curiously, there was no smell of cooking food.

They waited and waited. They began to be restless, and they were very hungry. Every man there had eaten lightly during the day so that he would be able to do justice to the big dinner at Yasu's house. After a long time they called to Yasu, "Can we help you get it ready?"

"No thank you," Yasu called back.

Later they called again, "Yasu, could we perhaps have part of the dinner now and the rest when it is ready? We are terribly hungry."

"I'm sorry, but all the dinner is in one pot."

At last, when Yasu's friends could wait no more, they got up and went to the next room. They crowded into the doorway and then stood speechless. Finally they looked at one another and laughed until tears flowed from their eyes at the sight they saw. Hanging from the ceiling, higher than their heads, was a big pot. Under the pot, on the floor at their feet, was one very small lighted candle. Yasu was standing on a stool, craning his neck to see into the pot. He turned to them and said innocently, "I'm sorry, my friends, that the food is cooking so slowly. But wait a little more, please. I know a candle gives out heat. You told me so."

THE FARMER OF BABBIA

ETHIOPIA, SUDAN, SOMALIA: This is an Ethiopian version of a story that is popular in many parts of the Arab world. From *The Fire on The Mountain* by Harold Courlander and Wolf Leslau.

ONCE IN THE TOWN of Babbia there was a farmer named Tesfa. He was known as an enthusiastic but silly man.

One day Tesfa's wife told him they would soon have a baby. Tesfa was highly elated. Nothing like that had ever happened to him. But very shortly he began to worry about what kind of child they would have, and so he questioned his wife:

"What kind of child will it be?"

But his wife couldn't give him any kind of a satisfactory answer.

"Stupid woman!" he said. "We are having a baby and you don't know what kind! Well, I will have to go to the wise monk in the mountains. He will know."

So he took one of the young bulls from his herd and drove him to the cave in the mountains where the monk lived. The monk looked at Tesfa inquiringly.

"I come to you for information," Tesfa said. "My wife tells me we are going to have a baby, but the stupid woman doesn't know what kind of baby it will be. Please let me know the answer. I have brought you a bull for payment."

The monk took out his divining board, and threw seeds upon it. This was the way he foretold the future. As the seeds fell upon the divining board, the monk shook his head. Tesfa shook his head, too. The monk clucked his tongue, and Tesfa clucked his tongue also.

The monk took up the seeds and threw them again.

"Aha!" he said.

"Aha!" Tesfa echoed.

Once more the monk threw the seeds on the divining board.

"Ho!" he said.

"Ho!" Tesfa replied expectantly.

At last the monk looked up at Tesfa. He was very serious.

"The child your wife will bear will be either a boy or a girl," he said.

Tesfa clapped his hands.

"A boy or a girl! How fortunate I am!" he said happily. He gave the monk the bull and ran home breathlessly to tell his wife the good news.

And true to the monk's words, in the course of time a child was born, and it was a boy.

"What a brilliant man the monk is!" Tesfa said over and over. "How truly he spoke!"

Soon the time came when they had to christen

the child, but they couldn't think of a suitable name for him. When Tesfa proposed a name his wife didn't like it, and when his wife suggested a name Tesfa didn't like it. They couldn't agree at all, and finally Tesfa said:

"I'll ask the monk. He is so wise. The monk shall be godfather."

So he took another young bull from his herd and went again to the cave of the monk.

"You have been so helpful in the past, help me again," he said. "Please tell us our boy's name."

The monk brought out his divining board and threw seeds on it.

"Aha!" he said.

"Aha!" Tesfa echoed.

"Ho!" the monk said.

"Ho!" Tesfa replied.

The monk looked at Tesfa wisely.

"Well, what is his name?" Tesfa asked.

"Come close," the monk said.

Tesfa came close.

"I have the name," the monk said. "I will put it in your hands so that you won't lose it."

Tesfa cupped his hands and held them out. The monk leaned forward and whispered into them.

"Close your hands quickly, so that you don't lose it now," the monk said aloud.

"Yes, yes, I am always losing things!" Tesfa said enthusiastically. "Thank you, we are deeply indebted! May you have many children and cattle!" And holding his hands together, he turned and ran homeward.

When he came to a place near the village where the farmers were threshing their grain, he raced toward them shouting:

"I have it! I have it! How lucky I am! I have my son's name!"

But as he ran through the straw and chaff he slipped and fell, and as he did so his hands came apart.

"Now I've lost it," he shouted at the farmers. "See what you made me do!"

He picked up a threshing fork and began to sift through the straw and chaff.

Some of the farmers came to help him.

"What does it look like?" they asked Tesfa.

"How do I know? I hadn't even opened it," Tesfa said with irritation.

As they sifted through the straw, a woman of the village came by. She asked what they were doing.

Tesfa explained everything. The woman shook her head.

"It's simply ridiculous," she said, and went on her way.

"Is it really?" Tesfa said with amazement. "Oh, thank you!"

And he dropped his fork and went home. His wife was waiting for him.

"Well," his wife asked, what is it?"

"I got it from the monk, but I dropped it in the straw," Tesfa said. "While I was looking for it our neighbor came by and told me it was Ridiculous. So I didn't have to look any more. How do you suppose she knew?"